THE SECRET
INSIDE

Geoffrey Hayes

THE SECRET INSIDE

Harper & Row, Publishers

Library of Congress Cataloging in Publication Data
Hayes, Geoffrey.
The secret inside.

Summary: Patrick, a small bear, meets a mysterious
innkeeper who shows him the secret of his innermost
thoughts.
[1. Individuality—Fiction.   2. Bears—Fiction]
I. Title.
PZ7.H31455Se   [E]   79-8519
ISBN 0-06-022273-5
ISBN 0-06-022274-3 lib. bdg.

For Charlotte—
who has a secret inside

Patrick had a secret inside of him.

None of his friends could see the secret

and when they didn't understand, it hurt.

Mama Bear could warm him in her fur and hug
the hurt away, but...One,

two, three trolleys rumbled up the hill—and still
no Mama Bear—

then...here she was,

squeezing him close and calling him her
"Honey Bear."

At bedtime, she told Patrick: "When I was a little girl and my friends didn't understand me, I felt lost, like a raindrop in a storm.

"Then I found a spot in the woods that I called 'The Jumping-Off Place' because I'd think of all the wonderful adventures I might jump into. And after a time, I didn't feel lost anymore.

"Now you jump into bed, and I'll kiss you good night."

Patrick couldn't sleep. He sat outside his window and gazed at the forest. A strange parade of fireflies was winding its way into the dark.

"I wonder where they're going," thought Patrick.
He followed the fireflies down a tunnel of trees—

and up a grassy hill. Below he could see a
hundred sparkling lights.

And without even thinking—*hup*! He jumped…

and landed in front of a little hotel aglow with
the dancing fireflies.

Leaning out one of the windows was the Lantern Keeper. "There you are, Patrick," he said. "Come in, I've been keeping the tea hot for you."

The table was set with all the things Patrick liked: biscuits spread with jam, tapioca pudding, and for dessert—little cakes in gold wrapping.

"How did you know I was coming?" asked Patrick.

"Because I know all about you," answered the Lantern Keeper. "I even know your secret. I'll show you after tea."

Later, he led Patrick down a hallway lined with
many doors. They passed big doors, square doors,
round ones and small.

And way down at the end of the hall was a door with Patrick's name on it. The Lantern Keeper opened the door,

and there were all of Patrick's dreams!

"*That's* my secret!" cried Patrick. "No one will ever dream what I dream or feel what I feel because no one else is me."

Then they walked through the meadow singing
and laughing.

By the time Patrick said good-bye to the Lantern
Keeper, he had found a new warmth.

It wasn't Mama Bear's warmth. It was all his own… warm as the pumping of his heart,

or a meadow filled with dreams.